Dear friend,

Our designers put so much effort into creating every outfit, so that it is stylish, easy to cut out, and fun to play with.

We wish this book will help you to express your creative style through fashion design.

We would like to hear about your experience with this book. Feel free to leave us a review on Amazon.

Visit our website for FREE colouring step-by-step tutorials and printables: **lucky-designs.com/links** or scan the QR code below.

Enjoy hours of fun dressing the paper doll models in different outfits, thanks to this fanciest colouring book.

How to use this book:

Step 1

Cut out the dolls from the back cover.
On the last pages of this book, you will find two stand templates.
Follow the instructions to attach the stands to your dolls.

Step 2

Pull out the pages inside this book and colour the clothes using your favourite art supplies.

Step 3

Cut out the outfits. Dress the dolls and start playing!

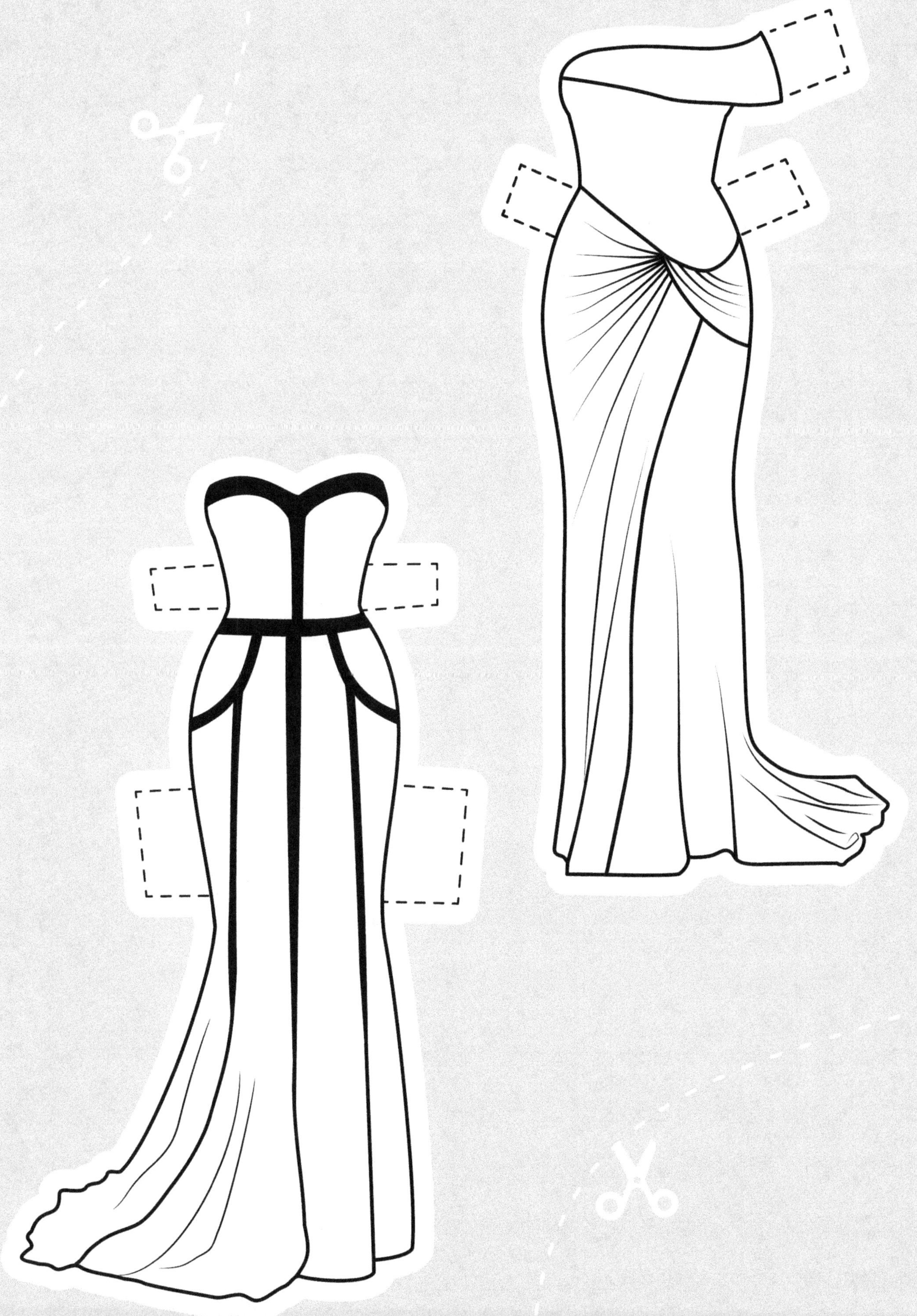

Paper Doll Stand

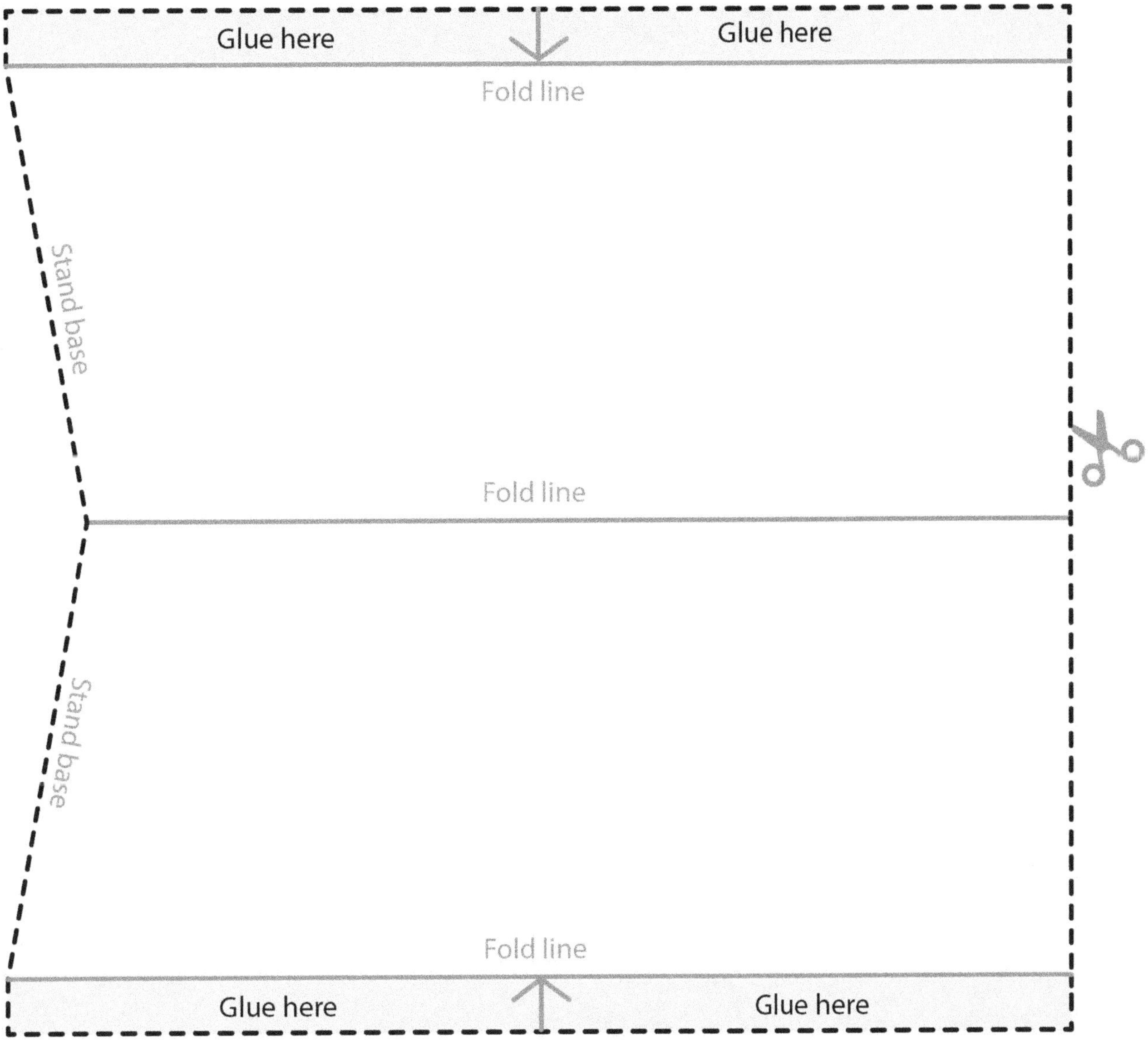

1. Cut out the stand along the dashed lines. Then fold the stand like this:

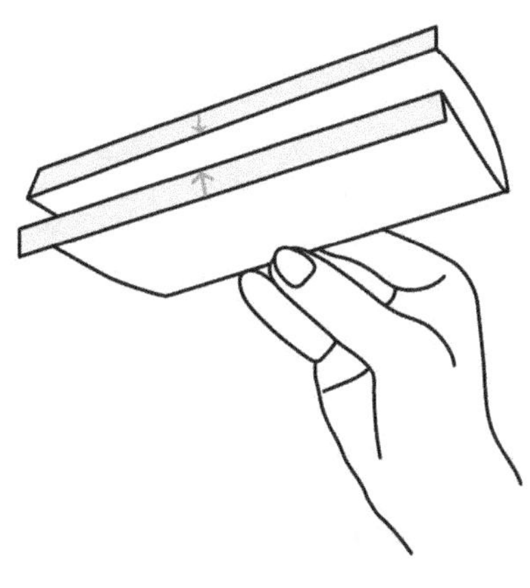

2. Glue the grey "wings" to the back side of your paper doll.

You can use tape, glue stick, or a white craft glue.

The doll will be a bit tilted backwards for better balance.

Once all done, you can start dressing the doll :)

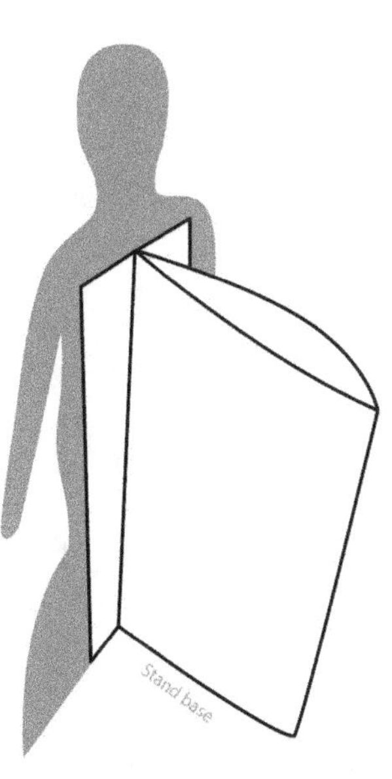

Paper Doll Stand

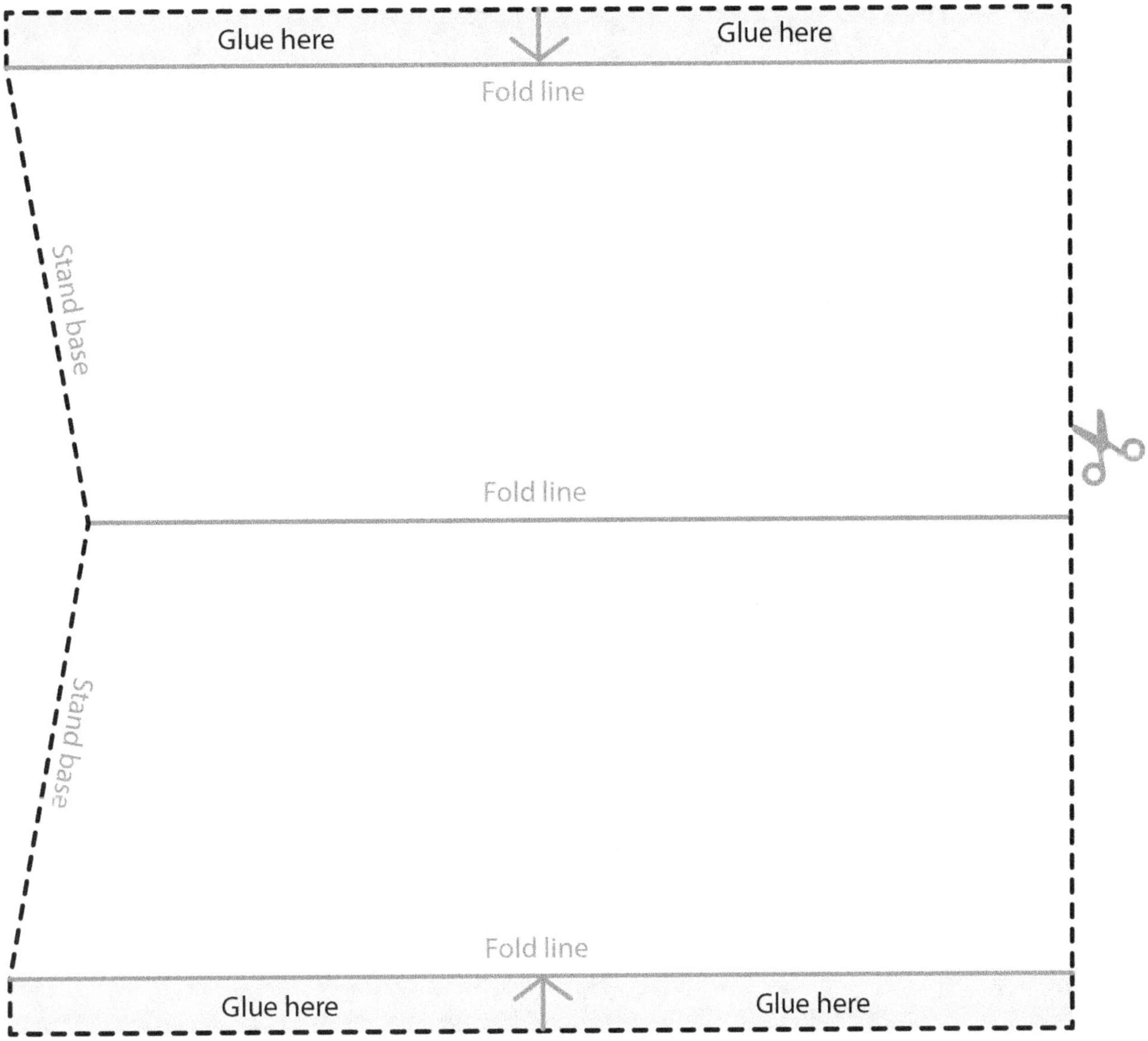

1. Cut out the stand along the dashed lines. Then fold the stand like this:

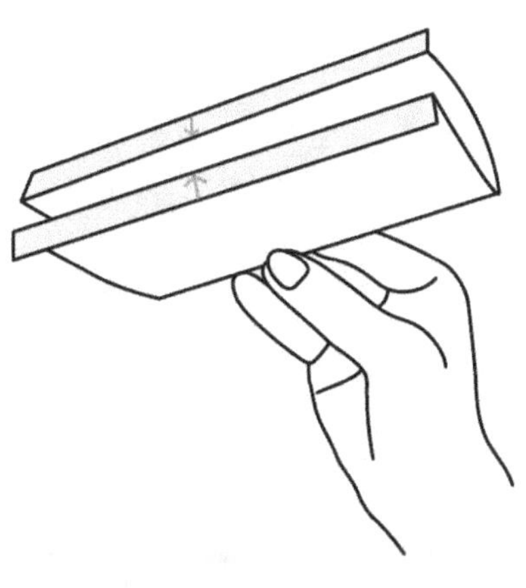

2. Glue the grey "wings" to the back side of your paper doll.

You can use tape, glue stick, or a white craft glue.

The doll will be a bit tilted backwards for better balance.

Once all done, you can start dressing the doll :)

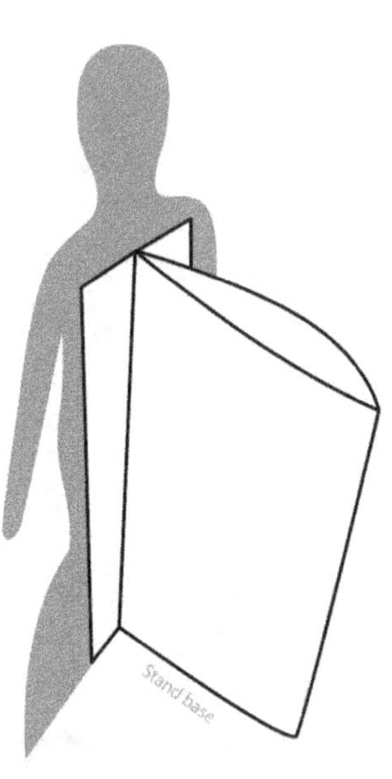

9 798725 686616